Written by Quentin Flynn
Illustrated by Bettina Guthridge

Contents

1 It's AIRHEAD! 4
2 A Life of Luxury 12
3 Headhunting 18
4 The VIP Room 25
5 Dismal Dudes 32
6 Horror Shock Rock 37
7 A Star Is Born 46

NELSON
CENGAGE Learning™
For learning solutions, visit cengage.com.au

Meet the Characters

Zoomer

The guitar player in Airhead.

Voxy

The singer in Airhead.

Snare

The drummer in Airhead.

Bartley O'Boogie

Airhead's manager.

Okahito

A Japanese butler.

Dear Reader

I'm sure all of us have dreamed of what it would be like to be a rock star. Behind our bedroom doors, when no-one's watching, we play our tennis racket "guitars" and sing loudly into our hairbrushes and ... oops, is that just me?

Anyway, I hope you enjoy this tale of super-stardom silliness. While you're reading, I've got a new song to practise! Yeehar!

Quentin Flynn
Author

The Airhead Gigs

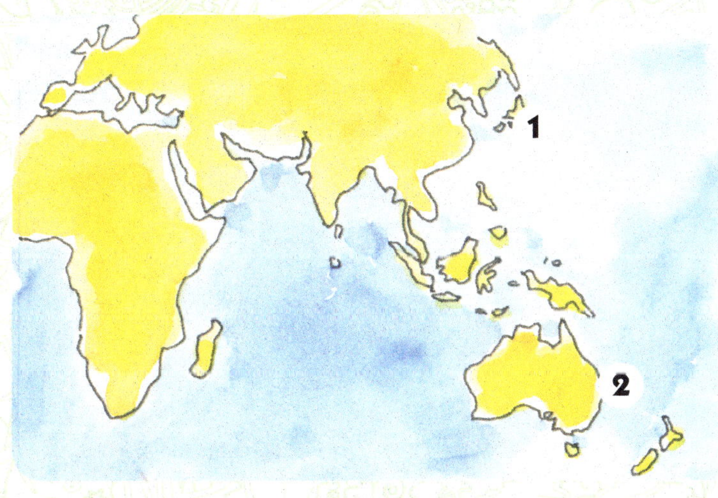

1. Tokyo, Japan
2. Brisbane, Australia

1 It's AIRHEAD!

Zoomer plugged in his cherry-red electric guitar. He wiped a bead of sweat from his forehead. The stack of amplifiers towering behind him buzzed. But not nearly as loudly as the huge crowd of Airhead fans, pressing towards the stage.

The arena was filled to capacity. Throughout the crowd, fans swayed on their friends' shoulders to get a better view of their idols.

A spotlight burst into life. An intense beam of white light lit up the rock star and his electric guitar amidst a sea of dark, pulsating shadows.

The crowd drew in its breath. Zoomer swung his arm in a wild arc. His guitar pick hit a string.

Ping, went the string.

TWANG!

bellowed the amplifiers.

The crowd went wild. They cheered and clapped. They threw hats, concert programs and inflatable Zoomer dolls into the air.

Zoomer's face burst into a wide, cheesy grin. "I love it when that happens," he chuckled to Snare, Airhead's drummer. Snare was dwarfed by a huge drum kit just behind Zoomer. "It doesn't matter what string I hit, they think I'm fabulous!"

Suddenly, he remembered he was supposed to be looking cool and suave. A deep gaze into the distance replaced the cheesy grin. It was a look that Airhead's manager, Bartley O'Boogie, had made him practise over and over again, until he got it just right.

"Just imagine you ordered a delicious lasagna for dinner, but they brought you peanut butter on toast," Bartley had suggested. "That'll give you the look."

It did. It worked every time. Zoomer gazed out over the crowd. His expression was tinged with sadness and disappointment. His head was full of thoughts of peanut butter on toast.

The crowd screamed with delight!

Snare looked at the drums in front of him.

"I wonder what that one sounds like," he thought, tapping a sparkly purple drum.

THUMP, THUMP, THUMP, boomed the amplifiers. The shockwave from the drums echoed through the arena, and the crowd started jumping in time to the beat.

"Keep going!" hissed Voxy, the singer. He held his microphone, pulled a face and closed his eyes. He was ready for the pain that was about to come.

"I hate this bit," he grumbled quietly. He dropped to his knees and hit the stage with a loud *crack*.

"OOWWWW!" he yelped. "Ow! Ow!"

A roar rose from the crowd and swept around the arena. It didn't matter to the crowd that they couldn't actually hear Zoomer, Snare and Voxy anymore. They were swept away by a tidal wave of sheer excitement – the excitement of being at a concert given by Airhead, the world's hottest rock band!

After the concert, Zoomer, Snare and Voxy piled into the back of a big stretch limo. Snare and Voxy fiddled with the knobs and switches that lined the limo doors. They watched in amazement as hidden refrigerator doors popped open, DVD movie screens whirred down, and different-coloured mood lighting filled the car. The limo edged its way through the fans who wanted a glimpse of their rock heroes.

Zoomer picked singed hairs from his head and sniffed them suspiciously. “Can we make sure that the fireworks are a bit further away next time?” he said.

Airhead’s manager, Bartley O’Boogie, squirmed around in the limo’s front seat. “The crowd loved that bit!” he assured Zoomer. “It was, like, you’re not afraid of danger, dude!”

"I'd be quite afraid of danger if I knew the fireworks were about to explode," grumbled Zoomer.

"Fearless, dude! Fearless but vulnerable!" said Bartley, nodding his head sagely. "Awesome! The punters will be queued up for days before our next gig, just to see you dicing with, like, death, dude."

Zoomer pushed a button on the limo door and a black-tinted window slid down. He shook the clump of barbecued hair out of the car. There was nearly a riot as fans scrambled for each strand of frizzled fluff that fluttered out from the limo.

Finally, the limo lost the crowds of fans and pulled onto the freeway. Zoomer, Snare and Voxy sat back in their seats and stared at the glittering skyscrapers and busy streets that whizzed past. "Where are we?" said Snare, looking puzzled.

Voxy looked at the name of the city he'd scribbled on the back of his left hand. "Tokyo," he said.

"And where are we playing next?" asked Snare.

Voxy looked at his right hand. "Brisbane," he replied. "Brisbane, we LOVE you!" he practised in his stage voice.

Snare frowned at Zoomer, who shrugged his shoulders. "No use looking at me, Snare. I haven't got a clue where Brisbane is."

"But you love them, dude," drawled Bartley from the front seat. "It's, like, being in love and not knowing where you're going to end up. That's, like, really deep, dude."

Zoomer, Snare and Voxy looked at each other.

"I think it's this one," said Zoomer. He pressed a button and Bartley's head disappeared behind a soundproof, tinted screen that rose behind the front seat.

"That's better," nodded the members of the world's hottest rock band.

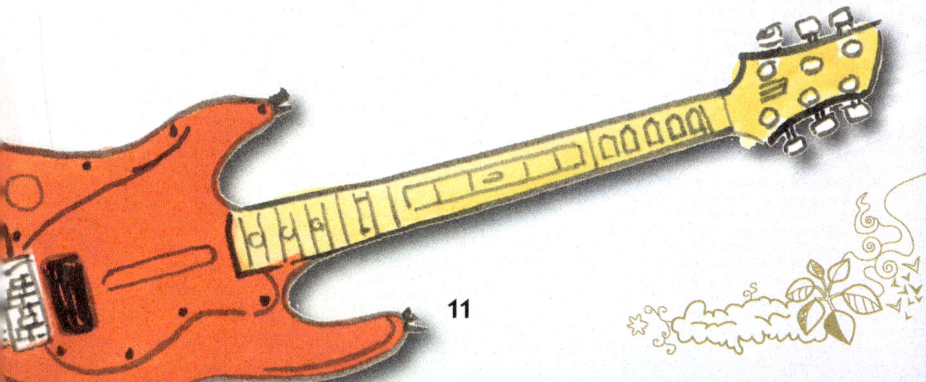

2 A Life of Luxury

Zoomer's luxury hotel room was so full of free goodies that he could hardly find room on the bed to flop down.

All day, while Zoomer and the other Airheads were at the Tokyo arena, a parade of hotel bellboys had been delivering armloads of free gifts. While Bartley O'Boogie's head often seemed like it was on another planet, Zoomer had to admit the contracts he signed with the people who put on concerts were "awesome, dude."

Every contract set out all the things that the members of Airhead needed to receive when they performed. As well as one million dollars in cash (which Bartley always put at the top of the list, next to a hand-drawn smiley face), there were electronic games, new sneakers, trendy sunglasses, pre-paid phones, basketballs, movie tickets, t-shirts and caps from local sports teams, and a souvenir teaspoon from each city (which Snare always gave to his mum).

ELECTRONIC

As the members of Airhead had found, being the world's hottest rock band meant no one ever said "no" to anything you wanted.

Zoomer was finding out why rock stars needed to have such huge mansions. He was running out of room to put everything.

In the last year alone, he'd got 234 t-shirts and caps from sports teams around the world (19 of which came from sports he'd never heard of). He had enough sunglasses to protect his eyesight from a nuclear explosion. He had so many sneakers that if they were lined up, they'd run ten blocks from his mansion (which was fine with Zoomer, because he had no intention of running the ten blocks himself).

He had a room full of phones that he could use to call people he didn't know in places he didn't remember. He had a room like a huge gumball machine, filled to the ceiling with basketballs. He had wallpapered his six bathrooms with unused movie tickets. He had hung shiny electronic game DVDs from a giant mirror ball in his garden to keep the birds away. And, unlike Snare, he had paved his driveway with a big mosaic of souvenir teaspoons.

"All this stuff ... and do you think I can find the minibar for a bag of peanuts?" said Zoomer, looking in every corner of his hotel room. He was starving.

He found the hotel phone under a pile of t-shirts from Tokyo's baseball team, the Yomiuri Giants. He dialled reception.

"Oh, no, sir, our mega-luxury ninety-ninth floor guests don't have refrigerators," said the receptionist. "They have a butler service instead. I will send our head butler, Okahito, to your room and he will ensure your every need is met."

Before Zoomer had even put down the phone, there was a knock on the door. He stepped over the phones and games that covered the floor. He peered through the spy hole on the door.

Outside, a tall, stately looking man with a fine pinstriped suit waited, his white-gloved hands folded patiently.

Zoomer opened the door.

"I am Okahito, sir. What may I bring you?"

"Um, can I have some peanuts, please?" said Zoomer.

"Of course you may, sir," replied Okahito. "How many?"

Zoomer thought for a moment.

"Three." He'd eat two packets now and save one for the plane trip tomorrow.

"Of course, sir," bowed Okahito. Zoomer watched the butler glide back down the corridor, before he shut the door.

"Wow!" he said to himself. "I've never had a butler before."

Shortly, there was another tap on the door. Zoomer found Okahito standing there, with a large silver platter on one arm.

"May I?" he enquired, nodding towards Zoomer's room.

"Sure," said Zoomer. He shot a glance around the room. "Sorry about the mess."

"Mess, sir?" replied Okahito. "I'm sure I don't know what you mean." He put the platter on a fine French antique side table (which Zoomer had been using for basketball bouncing practice), bowed, and left the room.

Zoomer hungrily went over to the table. He lifted off the top of the silver platter. "Oh," he said, peering at its contents. There were three beautifully polished peanuts, carefully arranged on an exquisite piece of bone china and, resting next to them, a pair of fine red lacquered chopsticks.

It wasn't quite what he'd expected. But it was, Zoomer reflected, exactly what he'd asked Okahito for.

"I must be a bit more specific next time," he mused, picking up the chopsticks and debating which of the magnificent peanuts he was going to eat first.

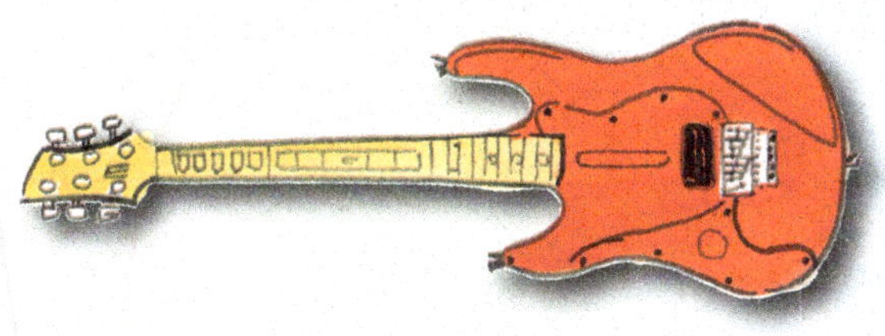

3 Headhunting

The next morning, the band gathered in the hotel's dining room for breakfast.

"A butler?" whistled Bartley O'Boogie. "You want me to add a butler to the contracts?"

"Not just *any* butler," replied Zoomer. "I want you to get Okahito. I want him to be part of the Airhead staff, going to all our gigs."

Bartley considered Zoomer's request, a process that needed lots of strange facial gestures.

"So, you want me to, like, be a head-hunter, dude?"

"A *what*?" said Zoomer.

"When you lure someone good away from their job, man," explained Bartley, "it's called 'headhunting'."

"OK," replied Zoomer. "But I want all of him. Not *just* his head," he added, just to be sure. There was no telling what Bartley would do once he had a thought in his weird mind.

"Why do you want a butler?" asked Snare, who was sucking on a *tsukemono* pickle. "Man, these are a lot stronger than cornflakes," he observed, pouring a jug of milk over his pickles.

"Last night, Okahito got everything I asked for," said Zoomer. "I started out with easy stuff, like peanuts. Then I felt like some ice-cream and he had nine flavours, all ready to scoop into five types of waffle cone. Then, all I had to do was pick up my remote control, and he was there with a silver tray full of DVDs to choose from."

"Awesome!" said Voxy, who was about to tuck into an extra-large scoop of something he liked the colour of.

"I need a butler," insisted Zoomer. "I'm sure all the other guitar players in the world's other hottest rock bands have got one."

"OK, dude," nodded Bartley. "I'll see what I can do. Hey Voxy, man, what's up?"

Voxy had jolted back in his chair. His nose had turned a hot shade of purple and his eyes were as wide as saucers and streaming with tears. "Ho, ho, ho, ho-o-o-o!" he gasped.

“Watch out for that *wasabi*, man,” advised Bartley, pointing at the green mound from which Voxy had eaten an entire spoonful. “That stuff is even hotter than pure mustard.”

Later that day, Airhead arrived in Brisbane. Zoomer sat on his baggage cart, watching the carousel at Brisbane airport clattering around and around. Finally, he spied his fluorescent pink suitcase.

“Allow me, sir,” came a voice from behind him. Okahito swiftly moved past the other passengers and claimed Zoomer’s suitcase. He took the luggage cart.

“Follow me, sir,” he said to Zoomer. “I have your passport. I’ll clear you through the VIP lane at customs.”

Zoomer was impressed. All through the nine-hour flight from Tokyo, Okahito had made sure he had nuts, water, napkins and eyeshades. He had peeled plastic wrappers from tiny blocks of cheese and mounted them artistically on crackers. He had adjusted the volume of Zoomer's headphones before placing them on his ears. He had expertly programmed movies and games on Zoomer's in-flight entertainment system. He had even asked the pilot not to talk over the intercom while Zoomer had been dozing.

"I should have had a butler long before now," mused Zoomer, as he followed Okahito towards the VIP lane. "How did I ever manage before?"

Zoomer, Okahito and the other members of Airhead were whisked through customs. In the arrivals hall, a crowd of fans was waiting. An excited cheer swept through the hall as Zoomer and his bandmates appeared through the sliding doors.

Zoomer couldn't resist swinging his arm in a wild arc, twanging the imaginary string of an imaginary electric guitar. The crowd yelled even louder.

"I don't even need an instrument," he grinned at Voxy and Snare, who were busy signing autographs.

Okahito expertly steered Zoomer through the crowd and towards the exit marked "Limos". Outside, he snapped his fingers and a giant limo the colour of vanilla ice-cream purred to the kerb.

Okahito opened the door and bowed.

"Please, sir," he said. "I'll put your suitcase in the boot."

Suddenly, Zoomer had a thought. "Okahito! You got my suitcase – but what about your suitcase?"

"Oh, I don't need a suitcase, sir. I carry all I need," smiled Okahito, tapping his suit pocket. "Don't worry."

Zoomer slid across the limo seat and was soon joined by Voxy and Snare. Bartley O'Boogie hopped in the front seat. He turned to the band. "The concert's tomorrow," he said, "Tonight, you have the night off."

"Cool," said Voxy. "Where are we again?"

"Brisbane, dude," replied Bartley. Voxy found a pen in the seat pocket in front of him, and drew a big tick next to the word "Brisbane" scrawled on his hand.

"Brisbane," he practised. "Brisbane, we LOVE you!"

Grand Hotel
THE GRAND HOTEL

4 The VIP Room

Somehow, Okahito had managed to get to the band's hotel first. He had already made sure that everyone was checked in.

When the vanilla ice-cream limo pulled up at the hotel, he was waiting. "This way, sirs," said Okahito, bowing to Zoomer, Snare and Voxy. "I'll have your suitcases sent up."

Once Voxy and Snare had found their rooms, Okahito took Zoomer towards a door marked "VIP Room".

"I had a word to the check-in desk," said Okahito. "I explained that you would require nothing but the best, sir." He swiped a card through the security lock, and the door clicked open. Zoomer was amazed by what he saw.

The view across Brisbane city and the river through the floor-to-ceiling windows was magnificent.

Fresh flowers were everywhere. A giant spa bath, brimming with bubbles, whirred out on the balcony. An enormous TV, the size of a ping pong table, was showing Zoomer's favourite cartoon show. And, in the middle of the cool marble floor, sat a gleaming grand piano.

Getting a butler, reflected Zoomer, was the best move he'd ever made!

"Is everything OK, sir?" enquired Okahito.

"Uh huh," nodded Zoomer, making a loud *ker-plink* sound on the piano keyboard.

A bell boy arrived with the fluorescent pink suitcase. Okahito set about arranging baseball caps, hanging shirts and placing neatly folded singlets and underpants in drawers in Zoomer's bedroom.

Zoomer wandered in. "I don't suppose ... " he started.

"Right here," said Okahito, holding up a fresh pair of bathers.

"Cool!" said Zoomer. He went to get changed. A minute later, there was a huge splash, as Zoomer

cannon-balled into the spa pool. A mist of frothy bubbles floated across Brisbane's skyline.

"Hey, Okahito," he called a few moments later. "Can you ... ?"

"Yes, sir," said Okahito, startling the rock star. He'd appeared out on the balcony without Zoomer even noticing.

"I need a ... " started Zoomer, but before he could finish, Okahito handed him one of the phones from the hotel room.

"Oh," said Zoomer. "Yes, that's what I wanted."

"I've already dialled, sir," said Okahito.

"Hello?" came a voice from the receiver.

"Snare!" replied Zoomer. "Get Voxy and come on over. Bring your bathers! You have to see this!"

Zoomer, Snare and Voxy sat in the spa pool, gazing over Brisbane. Inside, Okahito mixed strawberry and mango cocktails and decorated them with toothpick-sized umbrellas.

In the distance, far below, Zoomer watched the tiny figures of people hurrying up and down the streets. Then, he spotted a doughnut shop.

"Mmmm," he said. "I feel like a custard and maple syrup doughnut."

"Chocolate and banana," said Snare dreamily. "They're my favourite."

"Mmmm. Whipped cream and apricot jam," added Voxy.

Zoomer turned around. "Okahito," he said. "I don't suppose you'd mind ... ?"

"Not at all, sir," replied Okahito.

"Get us a box!" suggested Snare.

"A box of each sort!" added Voxy. "A box of each sort EACH! That way, you won't have to go back when we run out."

"Very well, sirs," nodded Okahito. "Anything else?"

The members of Airhead thought for a moment.

"I like barbecued banana prawns," said Snare. "Anyone else want some?" Zoomer and Voxy nodded eagerly.

"And if you can find some deep-fried wontons, that would be cool," said Voxy hopefully.

"Chips," said Zoomer. "I'm hanging out for a big bowl of hot, salty chips.

"With mayonnaise!" piped up Snare. "I love dunking hot chips into mayonnaise!"

"And three triple-chocolate milkshakes!" said Zoomer. "Make sure they use full-fat ice-cream."

"And none of that watery green low-fat milk," frowned Voxy.

"No, in fact, make sure they mix them with just cream!" giggled Snare.

"Naturally, sir," nodded Okahito.

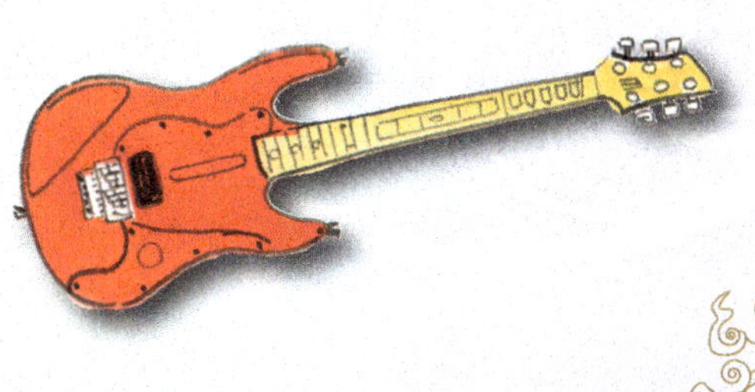

As the long, hot Brisbane afternoon wore on, Airhead's guitarist, drummer and singer soaked up the Queensland sunshine. Like a good butler, Okahito obliged their every wish. Soon, the balcony was littered with doughnut boxes, milkshake cartons, prawn tails and wonton crumbs. From time to time, the Airheads thought of new things that Okahito could find for them. By the time the sun set, deep-fried chicken wings, leftover cheese triangles, crispy battered chocolate bars and every kind of caramel lolly available in Brisbane were added to the debris strewn around the spa pool.

"Hey, it's getting dark," burped Snare as night fell over the city.

"I guess we'd better head back to our rooms," sighed Voxy, who was watching his belly bob up and down in the water.

Okahito appeared beside the spa pool. He leant over and flicked a switch. Suddenly, a hundred lights lit up the water in a rainbow of colour.

"Wow," said Zoomer, watching electric rainbows swirling around the soapy pool. "We could stay here all night!"

Snare and Voxy looked at each other, but before they could say a word, Okahito went and got three goose-down pillows from inside the VIP room.

Zoomer, Snare and Voxy shrugged.

It sure was tough being a member of the world's hottest rock band. But someone had to do it. They sighed. It might as well be them!

5 Dismal Dudes

Zoomer's stomach felt like a circus balloon that had been inflated to bursting point. A green circus balloon, he decided, as he struggled to get out of the slippery soap-sud-laden spa pool.

While he was trying to decide which one of the three marble bathrooms he would head for, he noticed a clock on the wall.

"THREE-THIRTY!" he gasped in alarm. "We can't have been asleep in that spa pool for fifteen hours!"

But they had. Before they'd retired at midnight the previous night, the band members had told Okahito that they should not be disturbed. And, as always, he had followed their wishes to the letter. Now they only had four hours until the concert began!

Zoomer heard a soft lilting sound coming from the kitchen of the room. He stumbled across the room and stared into the kitchen.

Okahito was perched serenely on a stool, playing a small flute. When he saw Zoomer lurching against the door frame, he stood up. “I hope my zen flute didn’t awaken you, sir?” he said, slipping the flute into his suit pocket.

“Your what?” said Zoomer.

“My zen flute. My *shakuhachi*. It helps me to meditate.”

“Er, no,” said Zoomer, whose gurgling tummy gave him an urgent reminder of where he had originally been heading. “Hold on just a moment,” he groaned.

Zoomer got to the bathroom. With a rising feeling of panic, he wondered how on earth he would get ready for the concert in time for tonight. Suddenly, the phone next to the hand basin shrilled. He just about fell off the toilet.

“Hello?” said Zoomer weakly.

“Dude!” came Bartley’s voice. “I hope you guys haven’t forgotten we’ve got to be at, like, the arena, man. I didn’t see you at breakfast or lunch. I hope you guys are OK?”

"We're fine," mumbled Zoomer. "We'll be there."

"Awe-some!" said Bartley, sounding relieved. "We'll see you at the arena in a few hours, dude." The phone went dead.

Zoomer washed his hands and stumbled out to see Okahito bowing by the door to Zoomer's bedroom.

"I hope you don't mind, sir," he said, "but I took the liberty of selecting a baseball cap for you. I thought it would save some time."

"Thanks!" said Zoomer. "Where are Snare and Voxy?"

"I woke them up and took them back to their rooms, sir," said Okahito. "Everything is taken care of."

Zoomer pulled on the maroon and yellow cap that Okahito had selected from the local sports teams' merchandise he'd arranged to be sent up.

"Thanks, Okahito," he said, feeling a little more relieved.

"My pleasure, sir," said Okahito.

Zoomer's butler, of course, made sure that Zoomer and his bandmates got to the arena in time for the evening's concert.

"Sit up in front," said Zoomer to Okahito. Bartley's already at the arena, so there's a spare seat."

"As you wish, sir," replied Okahito.

The band members squeezed into the back seat of the limo, each of them feeling queasy and uncomfortable. They were all regretting their indulgence on the balcony overlooking the city skyline last night. But, with an alarmed glance at each other, there was something else they all realised that was wrong.

Bartley, when he saw them, would not be pleased.

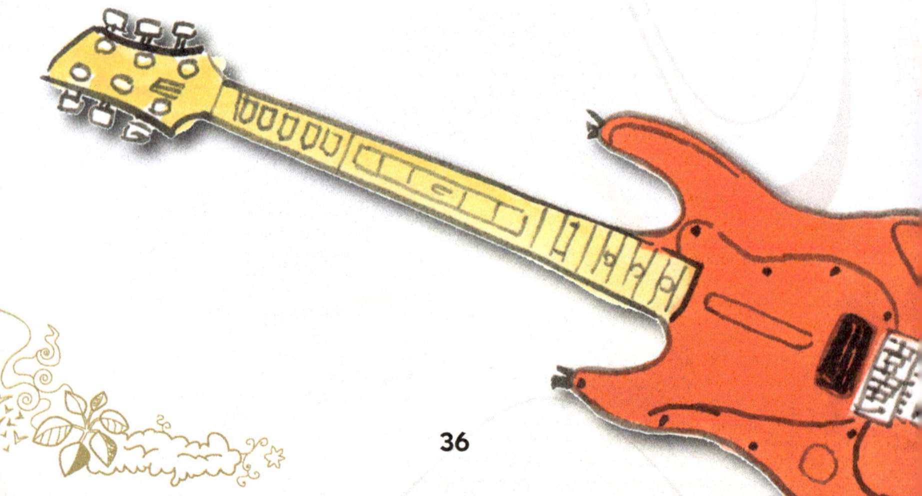

6 Horror Shock Rock

"Dudes!" gasped Bartley. His head bobbed up and down like a ping pong spectator as he examined each of the band members. "Did we, like, decide on a new image or what?"

After fifteen hours in a spa pool, Zoomer, Snare and Voxy's skin was puckered and shrivelled like wrinkly, ripe passionfruits.

"Yeah, it's like horror shock rock, dudes," pondered Bartley. Then he whistled at Airhead's bare midriffs, belly buttons exposed as their t-shirts rode up over their big, grotesque bellies. "Combined with glam girl-band fashion. Yeah!"

"Well, not exactly ... " mumbled Zoomer in embarrassment.

"Hey, dudes, I get it," nodded Bartley approvingly. "Everyone's doing the bare midriff these days. But you guys have taken it, like, one *big* step further!"

A huge burp erupted from Snare's newly fashionable midriff, and his belly button quivered as it gurgled upwards.

The aroma of old prawns mixed with stale chocolate milkshake and chicken wings well past their use-by date enveloped the dressing room backstage.

"Ten minutes, dudes," warned Bartley, heading quickly for the door. "Then we're live!"

The members of Airhead glumly found themselves three chairs and stared at each other.

"Anything you need, sir?" said Okahito helpfully, as he finished polishing Zoomer's guitar pick.

"No, thanks, Okahito," winced Zoomer, as he tried to rebalance his stomach on his lap.

"I'll be just offstage, sir, if you need any help, sir," bowed Okahito. "I'm sure it will be a wonderful concert, sir."

"Wonderful," echoed Voxy, as Okahito silently disappeared.

Finally, Zoomer heaved himself out of the chair.

STAGE DOOR

The dull roar of the crowd was growing louder and louder with every minute as showtime approached. "Well, the show must go on," he said half-heartedly.

"It's a pity your butler's gone," said Snare dejectedly. "He could have wheeled us to the stage on luggage carts. I can hardly stand up."

"Lucky you're the drummer then," remarked Voxy. "At least you get to sit down for the whole show."

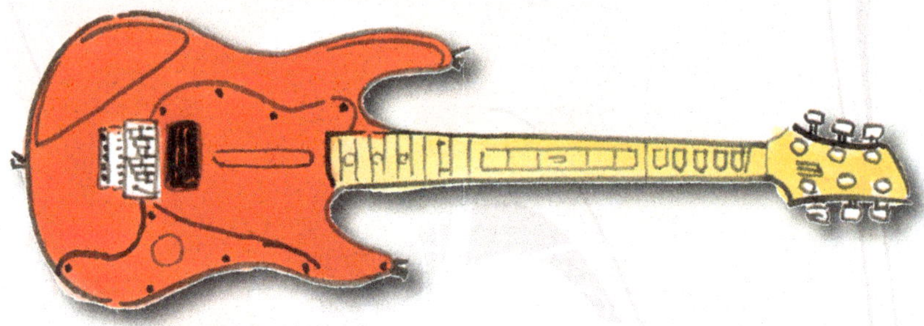

When Zoomer, Snare and Voxy finally made their way up from the dressing room, the stage had been darkened and there was a buzz of excited expectation swirling around the arena. The members of Airhead slowly picked their way around the amplifiers and stage lights and took their places.

"Ladies and gentlemen!" boomed Bartley O'Boogie's voice over the loudspeakers. "Now! The moment you've been waiting for."

Twenty thousand fans drew in their breath.

"It's AIRHEAD!"

A tremendous cheer rose from the crowd as flashlights suddenly bathed Zoomer, Snare and Voxy in brilliant white-hot light. Zoomer plugged in his cherry-red electric guitar and nervously wiped a bead of sweat from his forehead. The stack of amplifiers towering behind him buzzed. In front of him, all he could see was a sea of dark, pulsating shadows.

"Just remember," called Snare. "It doesn't matter what string you hit, they'll think you're fabulous."

Zoomer gulped and swung his arm in a wild arc. Instantly, the guitar pick he held in his puckered fingers flew out into the audience and, instead of twanging a string, his empty hand thwacked into his belly and bounced off with a quiver.

"Oops," he said.

Snare leaned forward, but his oversized belly wedged itself under a snare drum that toppled over with a loud clatter. Voxy, who knew he had to do something, reached out for the microphone stand – but his midriff reached it before his hand did, making the microphone sway wildly in front of him. Finally, he caught the microphone and cleared his throat. He looked at the back of his hand – and with a feeling of dread, realised that the spa bath had soaked off the name of the city he'd written there.

"Err ... B–B–," he stammered, trying to remember where he was. "Whoever you are, we LOVE you!"

The crowd fell silent.

Zoomer stood on stage, feeling as completely alone as anyone in front of a crowd of 20 000 people could. He wondered what to do next. Then he heard a voice. "Sir!"

Zoomer whirled around and gazed into the gloom offstage. A few people in the crowd began to boo. Someone started a slow clap.

“What?” hissed Zoomer.

“Do you need anything, sir?” came Okahito’s voice.

“I need some help!” wailed Zoomer, sensing that the crowd was becoming more and more disgruntled.

“As you wish, sir,” replied Okahito.

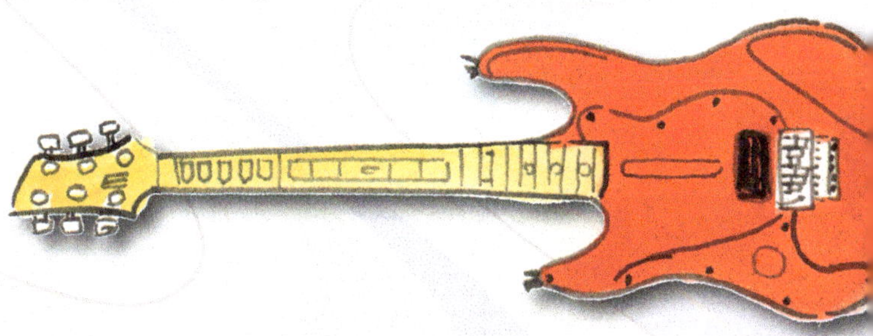

The slow clapping turned into an angry stomping, as 20 000 people wondered why they’d just paid huge amounts of money for three people who clearly didn’t know how to put on a show.

Suddenly, just as Zoomer had made up his mind to make a dash for it, a soft lilting sound streamed out of the loudspeakers and swirled around the arena.

Then, to Zoomer’s disbelief, Okahito serenely strolled onto the stage, bowing and playing his *shakuhachi*.

The crowd was instantly entranced. What was this beautiful, melodic instrument? And who was this stately man in a smartly pressed pinstriped suit?

As Okahito played a particularly haunting note, the crowd burst into applause, and the arena was in uproar. The melody of the *shakuhachi* could hardly be heard above the noise of the rapturous crowd.

Okahito stopped playing for a second and turned to Zoomer, Snare and Voxy. "It doesn't seem to matter what note I play, they think I'm fabulous!" he said in surprise.

7 A Star Is Born

"Dude!" said Bartley in admiration. "I'm signing you as the next major megastar, man!"

"Really?" said Okahito, who had enthralled the Brisbane audience with his bamboo flute.

"Yeah, dude, I totally get it. Japanese techno-fusion flute, man, it's like the next BIG thing!" said Bartley. "You name your price, man. Anything you want, I'll put it in your contract! "

"Hey, what about us?" piped up Zoomer from the corner of the dressing room.

"Don't worry about them," said Bartley, waving a dismissive hand at Airhead. "Last year's stars, man. Soon, they'll be playing elevator music, if they're lucky."

"But ... !" said Zoomer incredulously. "But ... !"

Bartley O'Boogie ignored the indignant noises coming from the corner of the dressing room. "Come on, man, what do you say? I'll make you a huge star!"

"OK," smiled Okahito. "But there is a special condition I'd like in my contract."

"Anything, dude!" said Bartley, pulling a sheaf of papers and a fountain pen out of his pocket.

"Well, fame and fortune are all very well," said Okahito thoughtfully. "But there is one thing I've been looking forward to for my whole life."

"Name it, dude," said Bartley.

Okahito plugged the microphone into his cherry-red electric *shakuhachi*. He wiped a bead of sweat from his forehead. The stack of amplifiers towering behind him buzzed. But not nearly as loudly as the enormous crowd of fans, pressing forward expectantly.

The arena was filled to capacity. Throughout the crowd, fans swayed on their friends' shoulders to get a better view of their idol.

A spotlight burst into life, an intense beam of white light isolating the rock star and his Japanese flute amidst a sea of dark, pulsating shadows.

Okahito took a deep breath. Then he blew.

Peep, went the flute.

PAAARP! bellowed the amplifiers.

The crowd went wild, cheering and clapping, and throwing hats, concert programs and life-sized inflatable Okahito dolls into the air. Okahito's face burst into a wide, cheesy grin.

"I love it when that happens," he said, winking offstage to his butler. "It doesn't matter what note I play, they think I'm fabulous!"

Okahito's butler straightened his tie and bowed respectfully. "Awesome," said Zoomer, gritting his teeth and smiling politely. He was still getting used to his pinstriped suit and new job. "Will there be anything else, sir?"